Word families:

"-ee"	⟶	three tree
	⟶	see

Sight words:

and	do	first	for
here	in	is	like
look	now	one	play
say	run	the	there
this	to	two	what
where	will	you	

Ready to go? Happy reading!

Don't miss the questions about the story
on the last page of this book.

This is Ian.

There You Are, OLIVIA™!

By Cala Spinner

Ready-to-Read

Simon Spotlight
New York London Toronto Sydney New Delhi

Here is a list of all the words you will find in this book. Sound them out before you begin reading the story.

Names:

Olivia   Ian

SIMON SPOTLIGHT
An imprint of Simon & Schuster Children's Publishing Division.
1230 Avenue of the Americas, New York, New York 10020.
This Simon Spotlight edition September 2017.
OLIVIA™ Ian Falconer Ink Unlimited, Inc. and © 2017 Ian Falconer and Classic Media, LLC. Based on the TV series
OLIVIA™ as seen on Nickelodeon™. All rights reserved, including the right of reproduction in whole or in part in any form.
SIMON SPOTLIGHT, READY-TO-READ, and colophon are registered trademarks of Simon & Schuster, Inc.
For information about special discounts for bulk purchases, please contact Simon & Schuster Special Sales at
1-866-506-1949 or business@simonandschuster.com.
Manufactured in the United States of America 0817 LAK
2 4 6 8 10 9 7 5 3 1
ISBN 978-1-5344-0371-0 (hc) ISBN 978-1-5344-0370-3 (pbk) ISBN 978-1-5344-0372-7 (eBook)

This is Olivia.

Ian and Olivia
like to play.

Ian will play first.

Olivia will say,
"One, two, three!"

Ian will run.

Olivia will look
for Ian.

Where is Ian?

Is Ian here?

Is Ian there?

Is Ian in the tree?

What do you see?

There is Ian!

Olivia will play now.

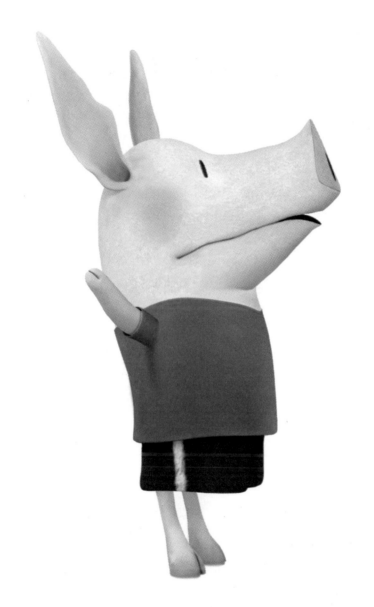

Ian will say, "One, two, three!"

Olivia will run.

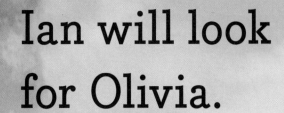

Ian will look
for Olivia.

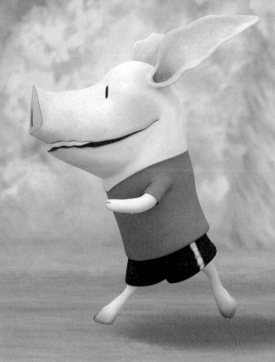

Where is Olivia?

Is Olivia here?

Is Olivia there?

Is Olivia in the tree?

What do you see?

There is Olivia!

Ian and Olivia
like to play!

Now that you have read the story, can you answer these questions?

1. Where was Ian hiding?

2. What do you think is a good hiding place?

3. In this story you read the rhyming words "three," "see," and "tree." Can you think of other words that rhyme with "three," "see," and "tree"?

Great job!
You are a reading star!